INDIA

KU-349-812

This book belongs to

DUDLEY SCHOOLS LIBRARY
AND INFORMATION SERVICE

Schools Library and Information Services

S00000671551

DUDLEY PUBLIC LIBRARIES

L 47986

671551 | SCH

          J 398·2
          IND

ISBN 81-7508-374-3

© India Book House Pvt Ltd, 2004

COVER DESIGN
Itu Chaudhuri Design

INDIA BOOK HOUSE PVT LTD
Mahalaxmi Chambers, 22 Bhulabhai Desai Road, Mumbai 400 026, India
Tel 91 22 2495 3827, Fax 91 22 2493 8406, E-mail publishing@ibhworld.com

All rights reserved. No part of this publication may be reproduced,
stored in a retrieval system, or transmitted in any form, electronic, mechanical or otherwise,
without the prior permission of the publishers.

THE ADVENTURES of
BIRBAL

as told by ROHINTON MODY

illustrated by SHALINEE GHOSH

IBH
INDIA BOOK HOUSE

THE WICKED BARBER

Birbal was a minister in the court of Akbar,
the greatest of the Mughal emperors who
once ruled India. His wit and wisdom
endeared him to both Hindus and Muslims,
and Akbar himself relied on Birbal for
advice on matters big and small.

But, the more popular a man gets, the
more enemies he makes. There were many
people who resented Birbal's success.
A group of minor courtiers turned quite
green whenever he effortlessly
solved a problem that they had
been breaking their heads over
for weeks. These courtiers were
always hatching plots to get rid
of Birbal or bring him into
disfavour with the emperor.
It took all of his cunning
to foil their schemes.

One day, as they sat
wracking their brains on

how to do away with Birbal, one of the courtiers hit upon a plan. The entire group agreed that it would work. So, off they went to the royal barber to put their plan into action.

'Hajam sahib,' (*hajam* is what they call a barber in India) said the courtier, 'if you will do us a small favour, we will give you a bag of gold.'

The barber's eyes gleamed with greed. 'What do you want me to do?' he asked eagerly. As a courtier whispered in his ear, the barber nodded. 'What a wonderful trick! It will teach Birbal a lesson,' he said, his face creased in smiles. 'Rest assured, I will tell the emperor tomorrow while I shave him.' The courtiers went home dreaming of their rapid rise to high positions in court, for Birbal was now certainly doomed.

All barbers love to strike up a conversation with their customers, and the royal barber was no different. 'Jahanpanah, Refuge of the World,' he said

to Akbar the next day, 'I have often wondered...' He stopped abruptly, razor in mid-air.

'Wondered what?' Akbar demanded. 'Go on, man, speak up. Wondered what?'

'Jahanpanah, has it ever occurred to you that you are doing nothing for the welfare of your ancestors?'

'What utter nonsense!' Akbar glared at the barber. 'My ancestors are all dead and in heaven. How on earth do I know what they need?'

'Surely you can send someone to find out for you.'

'And just how do you propose I do that?' Akbar asked incredulously.

'Arrange a thousand bundles of hay on the open ground outside the city. Then, a man that your majesty chooses should lie down amidst the bundles and more hay placed on top of him. The pile must then be set alight.'

Akbar stared at the barber as if he had lost his mind. But, unmindful of the emperor's look, the barber continued. 'As the smoke rises, the man will rise with it and go straight to heaven. Once there, he can ask after your ancestors.'

'I see,' Akbar said. 'And who do you suggest I send to heaven?'

The barber stroked his flowing, white beard and pretended to think. At last, he looked at Akbar and replied, 'It must be a man you trust implicitly. One who will tell you the truth about the state of your ancestors.' Akbar raised an eyebrow. 'And there is only one such man who comes to mind. That jewel among your courtiers, the wise Birbal.'

Akbar pretended to consider the barber's advice, but his mind was in turmoil. 'So, that is your game, is it?' he thought. 'Another trap for my trusted friend. Will Birbal be able to escape this one? I wonder who put the barber up to it.' Aloud he said, 'I like your idea. Birbal will go to heaven and find out about my ancestors. Now finish my shave so I can call Birbal and tell him.'

Pleased at having succeeded so easily, the barber stropped the razor and began to scrape the royal visage.

That very evening, the emperor announced his intentions to the court: '...and there is no one I trust more than Birbal to get me the truth,' he concluded. 'Therefore, Birbal, I want you to go to heaven and find out if my ancestors need anything.'

Akbar's words puzzled Birbal, but he hid his feelings. 'What a fantastic idea, Jahanpanah. What made you think of it?'

'Oh, I didn't think of it.' Akbar replied. 'It was the royal barber who suggested it.' The emperor looked at Birbal as if to say, 'That should be clue enough for you, my friend.'

'So,' Birbal thought to himself, 'it was the barber's idea. I will have to teach the rogue a lesson he won't forget for a long time.' Aloud, he said, 'Very well, Jahanpanah, I am willing to go. But before I leave, I would like to set my affairs in order in case I am held up in heaven. Would you, therefore, give me a few days' leave to do so?'

'Take as many days as you wish,' the emperor said. 'Meanwhile, let a thousand bundles of hay be collected in the open ground outside the city.'

Birbal hurried home and sent for a few trusted

workmen. He asked them to dig a tunnel from his house
to the open plot where the hay was being piled.

When the tunnel was completed, Birbal presented
himself before Akbar, ready to carry out his mission.
The next day, everyone gathered to see Birbal ascend
to heaven. He chose a place close to the mouth of the
tunnel, which his men had cleverly concealed with a
few bundles of hay. 'I will lie down here,' he pointed,
'and you can start piling the hay around me.'

In no time at all, there was a huge mound of hay
heaped on top of Birbal. The barber was given the
honour of setting it alight, since the whole thing was
his idea. As the hay began to crackle and burn, Birbal's
friends wept openly. 'Poor man,' one of them said,
'he was a good and noble soul, a real friend. How can
he come back alive?' Watching from a distance, Akbar
wondered the same thing.

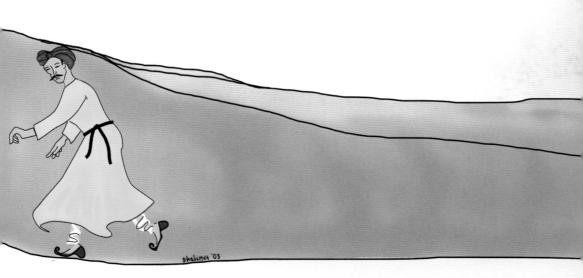

A group standing to one side, however, rejoiced. 'At last we have got rid of Birbal. Come, let us celebrate!' They did not know that even as they spoke, Birbal was racing to his house through the underground tunnel. He decided to stay home for a while and figure out a way to punish the barber.

Akbar expected Birbal to return to court quite soon. But the days turned to weeks and the weeks turned to months, and the emperor feared that for once his trusted friend had failed to evade the trap set by his enemies.

Six months passed. Then, one day, a stranger none of the courtiers recognized entered the court. A thick beard covered his face and long, straggly hair grew out from under his turban. He went straight to where Akbar was seated. The emperor recognized his friend immediately and was overjoyed to see Birbal's familiar, though rather unkempt, face.

'It is good to see you again, Birbal,' Akbar said.

'Jahanpanah,' Birbal bowed before him, 'I come straight from heaven.'

'How is everybody up there? How is my father?'

'They are fine and have all the comforts,' Birbal replied. 'Only one thing makes them unhappy. As you can see by my long hair and beard, there are no barbers in heaven. Your ancestors wish you to send them a good one.'

Akbar smiled. 'That should not be difficult, now that we know that the journey can be made.' With a twinkle in his eyes, he asked, 'But whom can we send?'

'Who else but the royal barber?' Birbal replied. 'Your father was particularly fond of him.'

'A brilliant idea,' Akbar said. 'I will send him post-haste. It will not do to make my ancestors wait.'

On hearing this, the barber began to quake with fear. He ran to the courtiers who had sought his help in doing away with Birbal. 'Help me!' he cried, 'Please save me. I am too young to go to heaven.' And copious tears mingled with his long, white beard.

'There is nothing we can do to help you,' the courtiers replied coldly, turning their backs on him.

Realizing he was trapped, the terrified barber took to his heels and was never heard of again.

THE BEGUM RECONCILED

Birbal's enemies continued to plot against him, and
whiled away their time by devising ways to humble
Akbar's favourite courtier. Before long, they hit on
another plan. This time they decided to make use of
Akbar's brother-in-law.

'Hussain Khan,' one of the courtiers said, 'as the
emperor's brother-in-law, you ought to be the minister
instead of Birbal.'

'I agree wholeheartedly,' Hussain replied, 'but the
emperor doesn't think so.'

'Why don't you ask your sister, the
Begum, to plead your case? Surely
the emperor will listen to his wife?'

'That is an excellent idea,'

Hussain said, looking at the courtiers in amazement. 'I wonder why I didn't think of it earlier.' Dismissing them, he marched off to see the Begum.

A few days later, the Begum was sitting deep in thought when Akbar entered her room. Seeing her so pensive, he said to her, 'Begum, you seem to be upset about something. Tell me your troubles; perhaps I could help you.'

She jumped to her feet. 'I want you to make my brother Hussain minister in Birbal's place,' she said.

'How can I do that?' Akbar asked. 'One needs intelligence to run the affairs of such a vast empire. And your brother doesn't have any ... I mean, enough of it. Besides, I must have a good reason to oust Birbal from his post.'

'Give him an impossible task to perform,' the Begum said. 'One in which he is bound to fail. Then ...'

'Very well,' Akbar interrupted impatiently. 'You suggest the task.'

The Begum thought for a while and said, 'When you are in the palace garden tomorrow, ask Birbal to bring me to you. He will not be able to carry out your order, come what may.'

Akbar sighed. 'I shall do as you ask. But I warn you, Birbal has a way of doing the seemingly impossible.' And, shaking his head, the emperor left the Begum's room.

'This time, my dear Birbal, you have met your match,' the Begum said to herself. 'Wild horses will not be able to drag me to the emperor tomorrow.'

The next day Akbar sat in the garden looking very troubled. Birbal approached him. 'Jahanpanah, something seems to be bothering you. What is the matter?'

'It is my Begum,' Akbar replied. 'Bring her to me now. Only you can do it.' Birbal bowed. 'But if you fail,' warned the emperor, 'you will no longer be my minister. I will appoint Hussain Khan in your place. That will please my Begum. Now go! Fetch her.'

As Birbal left in search of the Begum, he thought, 'My enemies seem to be at work again.'

A little later, he stood before the Begum, worry etched deep on his face. 'Begum sahiba,' he said, 'I come with an urgent message from the emperor. He is in the palace garden and he wants you to...' Before he could go any further, a messenger came rushing in.

'I have a message for you, sir,' he said.

'Speak!' commanded Birbal.

'I am sorry, sir, the message is for your ears alone.'

Birbal took the man aside and listened intently to his whispered message. The Begum strained her ears to hear, but all she could make out were the three words; 'She is beautiful'. The words startled her.

Moments later, Birbal turned to the Begum. 'The whole situation has changed, Begum sahiba. There is no longer any need for you to come to the garden to meet the emperor.' Saying that, Birbal hurried away, leaving a very worried Begum behind.

'What is going on?' she wondered. 'Who is beautiful? Perhaps my husband has found someone else to love and does not wish me to know. That is why he does not want me in the palace garden. But I am the Begum and no one can stop me from going there.'

So, her curiosity getting the better of her, the Begum ran to the garden. She stopped in surprise when she saw the emperor standing alone amidst the flowers and the trees. Akbar was just as surprised to see her. 'Why, Begum,' he said. 'I thought you were determined not to come to the garden today.'

The Begum looked annoyed. 'I was tricked into coming by your minister.'

Akbar smiled at her. 'You can't say I didn't warn you. But did Birbal tell a lie to trick you into coming here? If he did, I shall punish him.'

'Not really.' Sheepishly, the Begum described how Birbal had urged her to come to the garden and then suddenly changed his mind.

A huge grin split Akbar's face. 'Did you rush here only because Birbal asked you not to come to the garden?' The Begum looked down at her feet and remained silent. She did not want her husband to know that it was the fear of a beautiful rival that had brought her running to the garden.

Soon Birbal arrived to join them and Akbar beamed at him, 'Once again you have won, Birbal, as you always do.' He turned to the Begum. 'Now, my dear, do you see why I have Birbal as my minister instead of your brother?' The Begum looked crestfallen and Akbar gave a loud guffaw. Then, holding her close, the emperor left the garden. Birbal watched them go into the palace. With a shake of his head and a smile on his lips he, too, made his way home.

WHAT THE BEGUM
HELD MOST DEAR

One day, Akbar happened to be very annoyed with his Begum. He ordered her to leave his palace before nightfall. The Begum begged and pleaded, but the emperor remained unmoved.

'I have made up my mind,' he said, 'you will have to go. You may take with you whatever objects are dear to you.' And Akbar left the Begum's room.

Distraught, the Begum sank to the floor, not knowing what to do. Suddenly, she thought of Birbal. 'If anyone can help me now, he can,' she thought.

She sent for Birbal and explained the situation to him. 'He told you to take whatever was dear to you, didn't he?' he asked. The Begum nodded. 'Then this is what you must do, Begum sahiba,'

and as Birbal unfolded his plan,
the Begum began to smile.

When Birbal left, the Begum
summoned her attendants at once.
'Pack my belongings,' she
ordered happily. 'I am going
to my parents' home for a
few days.'

When their job was done,
she said to them, 'Now go to the
emperor and tell him I wish to see
him before I leave.' They did as they
were told and, a little later, Akbar arrived,
still looking grumpy.

'You wished to see me?' he asked
gruffly.

'Yes,' the Begum replied. 'I would
like you to have a last glass of
sherbet with me before I leave.
Will you grant me at least this
small favour?'

'Very well,' Akbar
agreed. 'But one glass
only, and then you must
be on your way.'

'As you wish, my lord,' the Begum replied, as she poured out a drink she knew would make Akbar very, very sleepy.

When the emperor finished the sherbet, he stifled a massive yawn. 'I must have had a hard day,' he said.

'Then rest awhile, my lord,' the Begum said, leading him to a couch. Akbar lay down and was soon snoring.

The Begum summoned her attendants again. 'Are the palanquins ready?' she asked.

'They are, my lady.'

'Good! Tell the palanquin bearers to lift the emperor carefully and put him in his palanquin. His sleep must not be disturbed.'

With the sleeping emperor in one palanquin and the

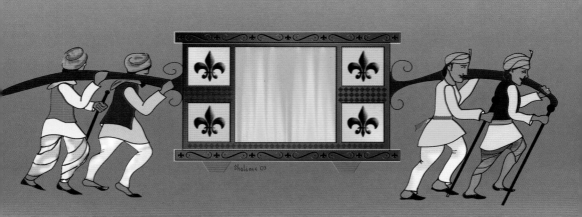

Begum in another, the procession left the palace. In a few hours, it reached the Begum's father's house. Although delighted to see her, he could not understand why the Begum had arrived so suddenly.

'I will explain everything to you later, father. Let me first make arrangements for the emperor's stay.' She had the still sleeping Akbar carried to a bed.

The Begum's father looked worried. 'Has he slept all the way from the palace?' he asked.

'Yes, but he is quite well, father. He will wake up in another hour or so.'

Sure enough, about an hour later, Akbar opened his eyes and stretched. 'That nap felt good,' he said. 'I must have been more tired than I thought.'

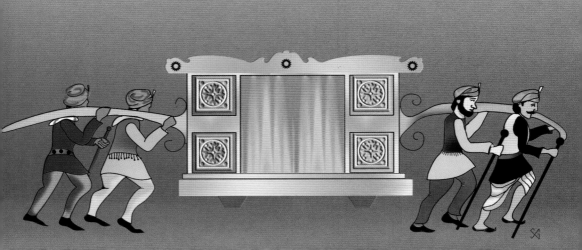

When he looked around, a scowl crossed his face. Just then, the Begum entered the room. Akbar glared at her. 'Isn't this your father's house?' She nodded. 'What am I doing here? How did I get here?' he demanded.

'Don't you remember that you ordered me to leave the palace, Jahanpanah?'

'Yes, yes,' Akbar said testily. 'But what does that have to do with my being here?'

'Why, you told me I could carry with me anything that was dear to me. And nothing is dearer to me than my husband. So, I brought you along.'

'What!!!' Akbar was astounded but the Begum stood innocently before him. 'How dare she make a fool of me, the emperor,' he fumed. 'Still, I must admit it was a brilliant trick.' Then he burst out laughing.

'I am pleased with you,' he said. 'That was nicely done. But tell me, whose idea was it?'

'Who but Birbal could have thought of it?' the Begum replied with a smile.

'True. But you were clever enough to ask for his advice.' Akbar pulled his Begum close to him. 'Come, forget about what happened and let us go back home where we belong.'

The Begum felt deeply obliged to Birbal for ever after.

BIRBAL'S VISIT TO PEGU

Hussain Khan was determined to replace Birbal as minister in Akbar's court. His sister, the Begum, was deaf to his pleas for help as she knew Birbal's true worth. Some courtiers, however, were only too happy to speak to the emperor on Hussain's behalf.

'Jahanpanah,' said one of them, 'we have had a Hindu minister for a long time. Would it not be fair to give Hussain Khan a chance?'

Akbar thought for a while. 'These people seem to be bent on getting rid of Birbal and making that fool Hussain my minister. It is time to put a stop to this nonsense once and for all.' He turned to the waiting courtier, 'You will have your answer in a few days' time. Now you may go.'

That evening, Akbar sent for Birbal and Hussain and announced that he had an important message for the king of Pegu, whose realm lay beyond the eastern border of Akbar's empire. 'I want the two of you to leave for Pegu as soon as possible and deliver this letter personally to the king. It is very urgent.'

Birbal and Hussain set out on their journey next morning. When they reached Pegu they demanded an immediate audience with the king. They said they had an urgent message for him from the emperor of Hindustan, as India was known at the time.

When the guard announced the visitors to the king, he became quite worried. 'What does Emperor Akbar want?' he wondered. 'Does he plan to conquer my country?' He told the guard to show in the guests.

Hussain Khan and Birbal entered and presented the sealed message to the king. When the king read the letter, he was astonished. 'How can this be? What does this mean?' He rolled it up nervously and turned to his minister. 'Make arrangements for their stay. See that they are comfortable, but keep a close watch on them. They should not escape.'

Both Birbal and Hussain were as surprised as the minister to hear that they were to be kept under guard.

Once the king was alone with his minister, he disclosed what the letter had said. 'The emperor of Hindustan wants me to hang his two messengers on the night of the full moon. Why send them to you? What do you think it means?'

'This seems very suspicious,' the minister agreed. 'Why couldn't Akbar hang them in Hindustan?'

'Perhaps,' the king mused, 'they are very powerful men at his court and Akbar does not want anyone to know that he has got rid of them.'

The minister looked worried. 'If these men are powerful, they will have a lot of supporters at the court. If one of them comes to power after Akbar, we may well be in trouble for killing their leaders. We must find out more about them.'

Meanwhile, Birbal and Hussain had a secret discussion of their own.

'I don't know the contents of the letter,' Birbal told Hussain. 'But from the king's order to keep us under guard, I think we have a serious problem.'

'I agree,' said Hussain. 'There are far too many guards for comfort. Birbal, you are the wisest man at Akbar's court. Please do not let any harm come to me. I shall be eternally grateful to you.'

'I shall do my best for I have no intention of rotting in a strange land. But you must remember to take your cue from me and repeat my words if necessary.'

Just then, the door to their room opened and the Pegu minister entered. 'I understand one of you is Birbal and the other Hussain Khan. Emperor Akbar has requested that both of you be hanged on the night of the full moon. Do you know why?'

Shocked as he was to hear these words, Birbal did not show his surprise. Instead, he replied calmly, 'Our emperor is always kind and just. Please carry out his orders.'

Hussain turned pale with fear but remembered what Birbal had said. 'Yes,' he agreed. 'You must hang us both on the night of the full moon.'

The minister was baffled and rushed to the king to report his conversation with the two emissaries. 'If we do not carry out his orders we will annoy the emperor of Hindustan,' said the king, but he was equally puzzled.

'There must surely be a reason why these two men are so eager to be hanged on the

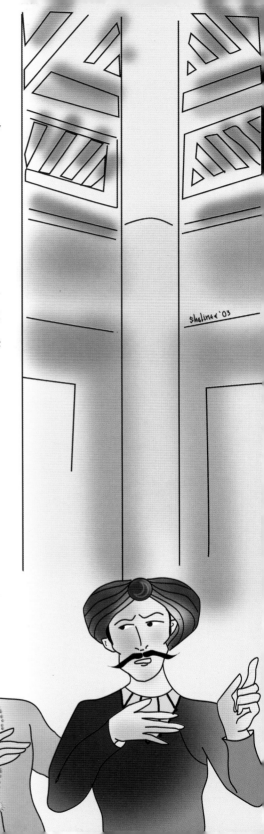

night of the full moon,' the minister insisted. 'And tomorrow is such a night!'

'What do we do?' asked the king. The minister shrugged helplessly and the two of them spent a very troubled, sleepless night.

Meanwhile, Birbal explained his plan to Hussain. 'When they take us to the gallows tomorrow, I will insist that I be hanged first. You must do the same.' Hussain nodded in agreement.

The next night Birbal and Hussain were led to the gallows where the king and his minister were waiting. 'Your majesty,' Birbal said as he bowed to the king. 'I was the bearer of the letter, so please hang me first.'

'I am the emperor's brother-in-law,' Hussain asserted. 'I beg you to hang me first.'

The minister turned to Birbal. 'If you tell us why you are so anxious to be hanged, we will hang you first.'

Birbal smiled to himself. 'Is that a promise?'

'Yes,' the minister replied.

Birbal spoke up loud and clear for all to hear. 'It is destined that whoever is killed here today will become the king of this country in his next birth.'

His words startled the king of Pegu. He called his minister aside. 'I do not want anyone but my son to be king of this country after me,' he said anxiously. 'I think we should write to Emperor Akbar that we do not know what crime these men have committed, and so we cannot hang them.'

The king's decision seemed to upset Birbal. 'Your majesty,' he complained, 'your minister is being unfair. He cannot now go back on his word.'

But the king refused to uphold his minister's promise. Instead, he ordered his guards to keep a close eye on the two visitors. He also threatened the guards with a painful death if either Birbal or Hussain Khan were harmed in any way or tried to commit suicide.

Early the next morning, Birbal and Hussain Khan were escorted to the border of Akbar's empire. 'They couldn't wait to get us out of their country,' Hussain laughed. In a few days, the two reached Akbar's court.

'Did you enjoy your trip to Pegu?' Akbar asked Birbal.

'Very much, Jahanpanah,' Birbal replied. 'We were treated with great honour and respect.'

'What about you, Hussain? Do you still want to be my minister in place of Birbal?'

'No, Jahanpanah,' Hussain replied as he bowed low. 'That post can only belong to Birbal. His wisdom is unmatched in this kingdom.'

Akbar sat back with a satisfied smile. Perhaps now his fool of a brother-in-law would stop pestering him about being made a minister!

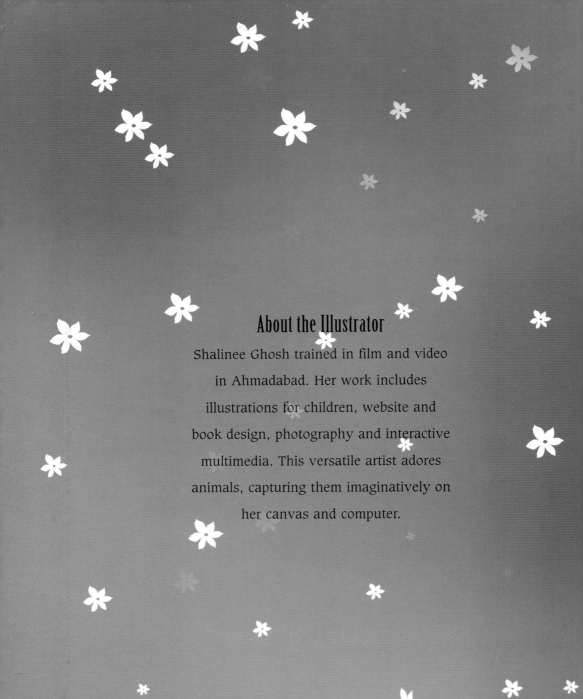

About the Illustrator

Shalinee Ghosh trained in film and video
in Ahmadabad. Her work includes
illustrations for children, website and
book design, photography and interactive
multimedia. This versatile artist adores
animals, capturing them imaginatively on
her canvas and computer.